STAR WARS

DROID TALES
EPISODES I-III

BY MICHAEL PRICE
ADAPTED BY KATE HOWARD

SCHOLASTIC

Scholastic Children's Books
Euston House,
24 Eversholt Street,
London NW1 1DB, UK

A division of Scholastic Ltd
London ~ New York ~ Toronto ~ Sydney ~ Auckland
Mexico City ~ New Delhi ~ Hong Kong

This book was first published in the US in 2016 by Scholastic Inc.
Published in the UK by Scholastic Ltd, 2016

ISBN 978 1407 16220 1

Book design by Erin McMahon

Printed and bound by L.E.G.O., Italy

2 4 6 8 10 9 7 5 3 1

Papers used by Scholastic Children's Books are made from woods grown in sustainable
forests.

www.scholastic.co.uk

MIX
Paper from
responsible sources
FSC® C023419

It was a time of great celebration throughout the galaxy. After a long struggle for freedom, the Rebel Alliance had destroyed the Empire's second Death Star. They had defeated Emperor Palpatine and restored balance to the Force.

"Yeah!" yelled Admiral Ackbar. "We are the bosses of blowing up Death Stars!"

Ackbar and the rest of the rebel leaders cheered.

All around the galaxy, people gathered to celebrate the downfall of the evil Emperor and his army. The Jedi and the Rebel Alliance had won the war!

In the Ewok village of Endor, Luke Skywalker and some of his Jedi friends were throwing a huge party. Some of Luke's oldest friends came by to help them celebrate.

"Yoda! Obi-Wan!" Luke gasped when the ghosts of his two old Jedi Masters appeared. "And . . . some other guy?"

The third guy shrugged. "I'm Anakin Skywalker – your father!"

Luke was confused. "Oh? You didn't look like that five minutes ago."

Before the Death Star blew up, Anakin Skywalker had looked an awful lot like Darth Vader.

A moment later, another ghost appeared. It was the ghost of Emperor Palpatine! "Hey, the old gang's together again!" the Emperor said, grinning. "It's all good – forgive and forget. Am I right, fellow ghost buddies?"

But there was no way the Jedi were going to let the ghost of their enemy hang out at their victory party. The ghost of Mace Windu appeared out of nowhere. "I'll handle this." He grabbed the Emperor, spun him around, and flung him deep into space.

"That's the second time this has happened today!" the Emperor screamed.

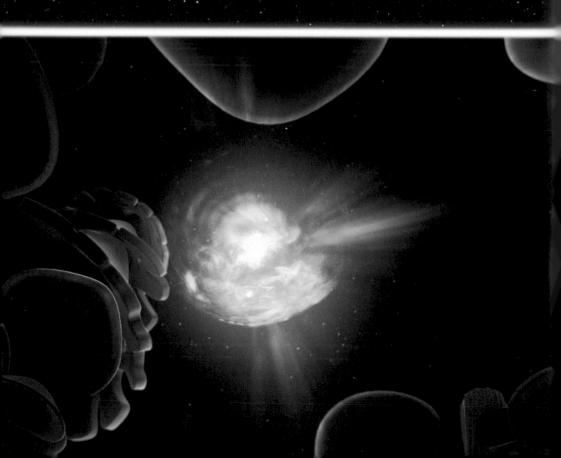

The rebel party in the Ewok village went on for hours. But by the next morning, it was time for everyone to get back to work. Now that the Empire had been defeated, the rebels would have to work hard to keep peace and rebuild the Republic.

But some were a bit slower to get back to work than others . . .

"What a shambles!" The droid C-3PO looked around at the mess that was left after the party. He and his droid pal, R2-D2, began to clean up.

"Lighten up, Threepio," said Princess Leia, rolling her eyes. "We just won a war. We're allowed to get a little carried away."

"You are right, of course," said C-3PO. "A celebration! And no one is more jubilant than I. Or Artoo, since, together, we have endured three decades of conflict."

"That's thirty years," Luke said, amazed. "So you two fought in the Clone Wars with Obi-Wan?"

"Indeed," C-3PO said proudly. "And with Master Yoda and your father, before he became Darth Vader."

Han Solo gasped. "Wait, what?! Luke's father is Darth Vader?"

C-3PO shrugged. "Everybody knows that. We learned it months ago."

GIVE ME A BREAK — I WAS FROZEN IN CARBONITE!

"Threepio, you must have amazing stories about those days," said Luke. "I'd love to hear them."

"I would be happy to regale you with my exploits, but I'm too busy right now," said C-3PO proudly. "Artoo and I are joining Admiral Ackbar on an urgent mission to free the lost Battle Droids of Mandalore."

"Your mission can wait a bit," Princess Leia said.

"That's fine with me!" Admiral Ackbar called out. He gently patted his new starfighter. "No hurry. It will give me more time to buff this little lady."

"Go ahead, Threepio," urged Luke. "Tell us your story!"

C-3PO looked nervous. "The truth is . . . I don't remember any of it. It seems my memory was wiped and—"

Beside him, R2-D2 beeped for attention. He held out a little memory stick labelled C-3PO MEMORY.

"You've had that all this time?" C-3PO gasped. "Well, jump to it, Artoo. Now I *do* have a story to tell!"

R2-D2 pressed the memory drive into the back of his friend's head.

Everyone gathered around, eager to hear C-3PO's story.

"Ah, yes," C-3PO said. "It's all coming back to me now. I can remember it as if it were yesterday. Let's begin at the beginning, when a Phantom Menace arose that led to an Attack of the Clones! Buckle up, it's a thrilling tale!"

After he droned on for a while, the group began to fall asleep.

C-3PO said, "Perhaps I should fast-forward to the day the unfinished me first laid eyes on Anakin Skywalker, the boy who would become Darth Vader."

THIRTY YEARS EARLIER

"There! You're half done." A boy named Anakin Skywalker had built his very own droid out of spare parts. The boy smiled down at his creation and said, "Now, what should I call you?"

"I've always been fond of Kevin," the droid replied.

"You are See-Threepio!"

C-3PO smiled weakly. "Best name ever."

Anakin's mother called out, "Ani, it's lunchtime."

Anakin cheered. "Yippee!"

"I made you peanut butter and jam on rye," his mother told him.

Suddenly, Anakin felt very angry. "I find your lack of white bread disturbing," he growled.

His mother stepped back, disturbed. "But . . . I have sourdough."

Anakin had no idea he was about to meet a Queen and two Jedi. But as he ate his lunch, Queen Padmé Amidala of Naboo was hurtling through space at lightspeed. Jedi Master Qui-Gon Jinn and his Padawan, Obi-Wan Kenobi, were in charge of keeping the Queen safe.

"All that matters now is that we break through this blockade so Queen Amidala won't be forced to sign the treaty," explained Qui-Gon.

"The shield generator's been hit," screamed Padmé. "I'll send the droids to fix it!"

All the R2 and R5 units on board were sent out to try to repair the Queen's broken ship. But one by one, they were all blasted into space. All except R2-D2! Soon, the ship was fixed.

"He did it!" yelled Padmé once R2 was back inside the ship. "The shield is repaired. Our troubles are over." A moment later, the ship began to twist and fall through space. Padmé looked at the two Jedi sheepishly. "But unfortunately . . . we are out of fuel."

BEEP!

BEEP!

The Queen's ship tumbled through space. It landed with a thud on a sandy desert planet called Tatooine. "Our rough landing damaged the ship's hyperdrive," Qui-Gon told Obi-Wan while Queen Amidala changed into a disguise. "Padmé and I will buy a new hyperdrive in Mos Espa. You stay here with the ship. Don't go anywhere."

"Yes, Master." Obi-Wan looked up at the ship and shrugged. "That, uh, won't be a problem."

A galaxy away, Darth Sidious was furious. "You are the worst bad guys ever! All I ask is that the Trade Federation help me destroy the Republic, but no! You fools let Queen Amidala escape Naboo!" Sidious screamed at Nute Gunray through his hologram. "This is my apprentice, Darth Maul. He will hunt the Jedi down. Then the Senate will feel the pain!"

I'M AWESOME! I'M HANDSOME! AWE-SOME!

"Cut that out!" Darth Sidious told his apprentice. Darth Maul pouted. "You never let me be me."

I PROBABLY CAUGHT HIM ON A BAD DAY.

Back on Tatooine, Qui-Gon, Padmé, and R2-D2 had reached the small town of Mos Espa. They found Watto's junk shop. C-3PO and Anakin worked in the shop.

"Hello," C-3PO said, greeting R2-D2. "You seem a friendly sort. My name is See-Threepio, human-cyborg—"

R2 rolled right past, ignoring him.

Inside the shop, Qui-Gon had found the part they needed to fix the ship. But he didn't have enough money.

Anakin told him, "I can help you! Bet on me in the big podrace tomorrow. I'm racing for my freedom. When I win it, you'll be able to buy a hundred hyperdrives!"

"Anakin," Qui-Gon said. "I think there's something unique and different about you. A power and gift I've never seen in a child." Qui-Gon could sense something special about young Skywalker.

HAVE YOU EVER CONSIDERED BEING A JEDI?

The next day, everyone on Tatooine was ready to watch the Boonta Eve Podrace Championship. The stadium was packed.

The announcer called out, "Coming to the starting line are today's racers: Sebulba in *Speed Demon*, Ben Quadinaros in the *Explode-at-the-Starting-Line-Mobile* . . . and Anakin Skywalker in *Destiny's Favourite*."

Up in the stands,
Qui-Gon, Padmé,
Anakin's mum and the
droids watched the racers
getting ready with great
interest. They all cheered
for Anakin.

"Victory is as good as
ours," Qui-Gon said.

Then the announcer
shouted, "Here's a fun
fact: Skywalker's never
successfully completed a podrace before!"

Everyone was much more nervous now.

ZOOM ZOOM!

But as soon as the race began, Qui-Gon's worries disappeared. "He's great! My good feeling about this . . . which had turned into a bad feeling about this . . . is now a good feeling again!"

Anakin raced around the podrace course. He was so fast!

The podracers zipped past desert bluffs. Tusken Raiders were hidden along the race-course, waiting to shoot at the racers as they zoomed past.

But Anakin darted from side to side, narrowly missing their fire!

Anakin raced through the winding course. One by one, each of the other podracers was taken down.

After a wild ride, Anakin blasted across the finish line first. "Skywalker is the winner!" the announcer yelled. "Looks like he has won his freedom from Watto . . . and he will now be trained as a Jedi by Qui-Gon Jinn!"

It was time for Anakin to leave Tatooine for bigger adventures. He had to say good-bye to his mum and his droid. Anakin jumped out of his pod to hug his mom.

"Good-bye, Ani!" C-3PO called after him.

DON'T FORGET TO WRITE YOUR NAME IN YOUR UNDERWEAR FOR LAUNDRY DAY!

As Qui-Gon, Padmé, R2-D2, and Anakin approached their ship with the new part, Obi-Wan ran towards them. "Master! Naboo is under attack from the entire Trade Federation Army!"

"I must protect my people," Padmé said. "Take me there!"

Qui-Gon shook his head. "I can't allow it. We'd be putting you and this young boy in extreme danger."

"Then maybe we could go to the Senate debate on the new spice mining regulations?" Obi-Wan suggested.

THAT SETTLES IT! EXTREME DANGER, HERE WE COME!

When they arrived on Naboo, Queen Padmé Amidala jumped into action right away. "Pilots," she ordered. "Take out that Droid Control Ship! We'll find the viceroys!"

"Hide in there," Qui-Gon told Anakin. He pointed to a starfighter. "But whatever you do, do not accidentally hit a wrong button that flies you up to the enemy's Droid Control Ship!"

"I didn't hit the button by accident," Anakin said as he fired up the starfighter. "I did it on purpose!"

Qui-Gon sighed. "Kids today."

Anakin raced out to join the battle in the sky. Meanwhile, Qui-Gon and Obi-Wan prepared to fight the Queen's enemies in the palace.

Their first challenge: Darth Maul!

"A Dark Lord of the Sith," Qui-Gon explained. "The Sith are an ancient evil enemy of the Jedi."

"That's an odd way to hold a standard one-bladed lightsaber," Obi-Wan whispered.

Obi-Wan gaped as another blade slid out of Darth Maul's lightsaber. "Two blades?"

"That is so cool!" gasped Qui-Gon.

"This is cooler!" hissed Darth Maul. He dived through the air, slicing LEGO bricks off the ceiling. The bricks collapsed on Qui-Gon, smashing him to the ground.

Qui-Gon's voice was weak. He called out to his Padawan from under the pile of bricks, "Obi-Wan . . . train the boy."

"I have to live through the next five minutes first," Obi-Wan shouted back. "But . . . okay!"

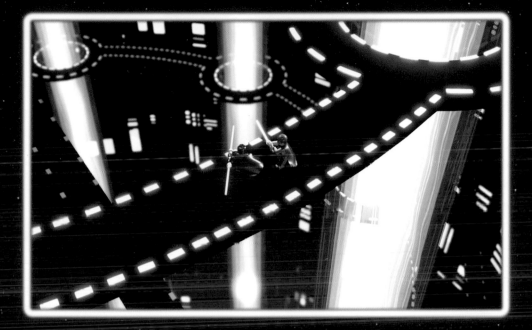

Qui-Gon was gone. Now it was one-on-one, Jedi versus Sith.

Losing his Master gave Obi-Wan the strength and focus he needed to battle Darth Maul. Obi-Wan leaped and slashed.

"Missed me!" Darth Maul taunted. "Nyah nyah nyah nyah nyah!"

But Obi-Wan hadn't missed. He'd scored a direct hit. The Sith was doomed.

UH, THAT CAN'T BE GOOD . . .

Meanwhile, in the Droid Control Ship, Nute Gunray from the Trade Federation Army was busy bragging. "It was so smart of us to control all of our Battle Droids from this one ship. Now no one can stop us!"

Then he looked out the window. A fleet of Naboo starfighters was streaking towards him, laser cannons blazing! Gunray covered his head. "Oh, boy!"

"Now, *this* is podracing!" Anakin cheered as his starfighter zoomed towards the army's Droid Control Ship.

"And *this* is blowing stuff up!" Anakin said, aiming his laser cannon fire at the control ship.

KA-BOOM!

Anakin was a hero!

"Qui-Gon would be very proud of you, Anakin," said Obi-Wan. "I'll be your teacher now that he is gone."

"Yippee!" Anakin cried. "Can I begin my training today?"

Obi-Wan shook his head. "I'm a little tired. How about tomorrow?"

"Don't make me destroy you," Anakin growled.

"Uh." Obi-Wan stepped back. "Today is fine . . ."

Chancellor Palpatine poked his head in from around the corner and said, "Anakin, I'll be watching your career with great interest."

Suddenly, the Chancellor's head swiveled around and he began to cackle. For a moment, he looked a lot like . . . Darth Sidious?!

HA HA HA!

THAT IS ONE EVIL LAUGH!

Queen Amidala took Anakin's hand. "You'll be a great Jedi, Anakin. I hope I see a lot more of you in the future."

ANAKIN
+
PADMÉ

IN THE PRESENT

"And thus began a love story that would lead to a secret wedding on Naboo many years later," C-3PO said, taking a break from his story. "Oh, it was so romantic."

Luke and Han both groaned. "Threepio, we don't care about a wedding," said Luke.

"Yeah," blurted out Admiral Ackbar. "Tell us how the Clone Wars started!"

C-3PO sighed. "Very well. It was quite a thrilling tale, and Artoo and I were there for it all."

CLONE WARS! CLONE WARS! CLONE WARS!

Just as C-3PO began to tell the next part of his tale, R2 noticed a hooded figure creeping through the Ewok village. He beeped to get everyone's attention. When no one listened, he tried to follow the intruder.

But C-3PO pulled him back. "Don't leave the stage, Artoo! This is your story, too." He waited until he had everyone's attention, then began his story again.

Ten years had passed since Anakin first became a Jedi. Padmé was no longer a Queen – she was now a senator and under attack by the Trade Federation viceroys. The viceroys' leader, Count Dooku, was a former Jedi. Dooku had gone over to the dark side.

Anakin and Obi-Wan were assigned to protect Padmé Amidala, but their job wasn't easy. To help protect her, the group often travelled with decoys.

"There's the shooter!" Obi-Wan shouted.

JANGO FETT: BOUNTY HUNTER!

"I've got this," Anakin said. He used the Force to help him deflect Jango Fett's darts.

WOW, I'M GOOD!

"The assailant's saberdart came from Kamino," Anakin reported back to the Jedi Council later that day. "I'll go there to investigate."

"No," Mace Windu said. "Obi-Wan will go. Anakin, your place is here guarding Senator Amidala."

"But—" Anakin whined.

Yoda shook his head. "No buts! Immature, you still are."

R2-D2 raced into the room, ready for action. "Not you, Artoo." Yoda sighed. "Him are, too. Are, too!"

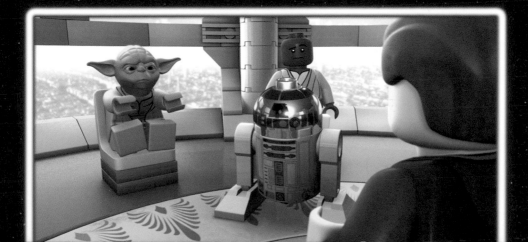

Later that night, Obi-Wan landed on Kamino. He used his comlink to report back to the Council: "I have arrived on Kamino. All looks normal . . ."

He flung open a door and gasped. He was surrounded by hundreds of clones!

"Hi!" the clones all called out in unison. "Are you our leader?"

Obi-Wan backed away. "I better report this to the Council."

"Bye-bye!" the clones yelled after him. "Call us when you need us!"

Obi-Wan rushed back to his ship to report his findings to the Council. But he didn't realize he had been followed . . . by the bounty hunter Jango Fett!

"Not so fast, Jedi!" the bounty hunter hissed.

Obi-Wan drew his lightsaber, ready for battle. "You'll pay for attacking Senator Amidala!"

"Try and make me!" Jango Fett laughed.

Meanwhile, back on Coruscant, Anakin and Padmé were out for a nice afternoon stroll.

"The Council said I'm just some hothead, Padmé. Well, I'll show them! They are *so wrong*!"

Padmé suggested, "Maybe if you tried to act more calm?"

"I AM ACTING CALM!" Anakin screamed.

As he threw his tantrum, Anakin's comlink chirped. "Anakin!" A hologram of Obi-Wan popped up. "I've run into a bit of trouble. The Sith and Separatists are building an army of Battle Droids. But I've got this! Do not come here to rescue me. I repeat: Do not come! Don't be a hero!"

Anakin looked at Padmé. "Clearly, I need to go there and be a hero!"

"I hope we're not too late to save Obi-Wan from those Battle Droids," Padmé said when she and Anakin landed on Geonosis. They had brought along R2 for backup.

Anakin gritted his teeth. "Either way, we're ready for a fight."

"Oh, dear," a voice called out from the shadows. "This is madness." It was C-3PO!

"Threepio!" gasped Anakin. "When did you get here?"

C-3PO shrugged. "It's a rather long story, I'm afraid."

Anakin, Padmé, C-3PO and R2 rushed off Anakin's ship and blasted open a door.

"It's a giant Battle Droid factory!" said Padmé.

"Cool," Anakin said. As they watched the machines hard at work, a bar suddenly swept past and knocked them all into the factory.

"Not cool!" screeched C-3PO.

"We're doomed!" Padmé yelled.

It was GAME OVER for the Jedi.

Anakin, Padmé, R2 and C-3PO were tossed into a battle arena to fight against hundreds of Battle Droids and Droidekas. Obi-Wan and the rest of their Jedi pals soon arrived to help them fight. But even with the extra help, they were outnumbered.

"I have had it with these blaster-firing droids!" Mace Windu grunted, swinging his lightsaber. Moments later, a Republic attack gunship flew into the arena. The ship was filled with clones, led by Master Yoda. They were saved! Saved by the clones!

While the clones helped the Jedi escape, Yoda took care of some unfinished business with Count Dooku. The two faced off, lightsabers drawn.

"Well, well, well . . . my old teacher," said Dooku. "It's time to teach you a few things."

"Wrong, you are. Back in session, school is!" said Yoda.

Yoda leapt into the air, doing backflips and somersaults. He was so busy showing off his crazy moves that he didn't notice Count Dooku escaping . . .

I'LL JUST LET MYSELF OUT . . .

"Good news, Lord Sidious," Count Dooku reported back to Darth Sidious a short while later. "The Clone War has begun."

"Just as I had planned," Sidious said.

"And here are the blueprints for your new super-weapon." Count Dooku handed over the plans for the Death Star.

OOH, GOODIE GOODIE GUMDROPS!

"And so," C-3PO said, "that is how the Clone Wars began. The stage was set for the fall of the Republic. And Artoo and I were right in the thick of it, weren't we, Artoo?" He looked around for his pal. "Artoo? Artoo-Detoo, where are you?"

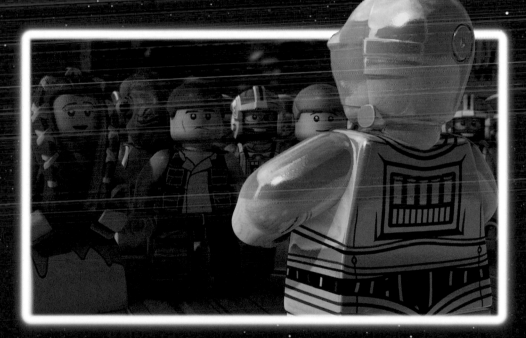

R2-D2 was gone.

R2-D2 had slipped away from the story to follow the mysterious, shadowy figure he'd seen sneaking around the Ewok village. When C-3PO yelled for him, R2 beeped in surprise.

The stranger turned around and growled, "You shouldn't have followed me!"

The hooded figure grabbed R2 and tossed him into Admiral Ackbar's new ship! A moment later, R2 and the stranger were gone.

MY BEST FRIEND IS GONE!

"We have got to bring him back!" C-3PO cried.

"I'll take you," Admiral Ackbar offered. "Quick — to my old ship."

C-3PO said, "Hurry. We must save Artoo."

"Hold on, let me just clear off the fast food wrappers on the passenger seat," Ackbar said as he tossed wrappers and rubbish out of his ship.

"I don't care about the trash!" C-3PO yelled. "Go! Now!"

Admiral Ackbar and C-3PO raced through the galaxy, trying to track R2 and the mysterious villain. C-3PO was desperate to rescue his friend, and Admiral Ackbar was eager to get his precious new ship back.

"Stay strong, Artoo," C-3PO wailed. "Your buddy's coming to bring you home!"

"You stay strong, too, *Daisy Mae*," Admiral Ackbar said. C-3PO gave him a strange look.

Ackbar shrugged. "That's my ship's name."

A short
while later,
they landed on
Coruscant.

"According
to my tracking
computer, the
stolen ship
was abandoned somewhere in this vicinity."
C-3PO looked around. He thought back to the
story he'd just been telling his friends on Endor.
"Oh, the awful things that have happened here
on Coruscant. Battles, the end of the Jedi . . . I'm
glad all that is over and we can get on with our
lives in peace and—"

C-3PO screamed as a battalion of Battle
Droids landed nearby. "Battle Droids! Hide me!"

"Take it easy, chief," Ackbar said, laughing.
"These old junkers were reprogrammed to be
useful. They're Garbage Droids now."

"Perhaps they have encountered Artoo!"
C-3PO said, perking up. "Garbage Droids, can
you help me?"

"Roger roger," the droids replied.

"Have you seen this Artoo unit?" C-3PO held
out a picture of his friend.

R2-D2

"Negative negative," droned the droids.
"You're no help at all!" C-3PO groaned.
"Sorry sorry!"

"I'll never find Artoo," C-3PO said sadly. He sat down and gazed at the picture of his friend. "Seeing those scary droids makes me miss him more. It was Artoo who destroyed that Battle Droid factory. It's a tale full of excitement and adventure and—"

"And my sweet ride is gone," Ackbar interrupted. The ship had fallen apart upon landing. "I'll never forget when I first saw *Daisy Mae* at the dealer . . ."

C-3PO blurted out, "A ship is just a machine! A droid is a person."

"Okay, fine," Admiral Ackbar said. "You tell your story."

C-3PO took a deep breath and began his next tale.

TWENTY YEARS EARLIER

Twenty years earlier, things on Coruscant were in constant turmoil. General Grievous had got his claws on the Republic's top-secret battle plans.

"This disc is all you need to crush the Jedi and win the war, General," Chancellor Palpatine told Grievous. "Take it to the Separatist Council at once."

"Yes, my lord," said General Grievous, chuckling. "Victory is ours!"

SECRET PLANS . . . AND I'M SECRETLY EVIL. MWAH-HA-HA!

KABOOM

Grievous ran towards his ship with the plans.
"My ship!" Grievous screamed. "Which was also my house!"
To keep Grievous from escaping, Obi-Wan had blown up the general's ship! Obi-Wan turned to his army of clones. "After him!"

OOPSIE!

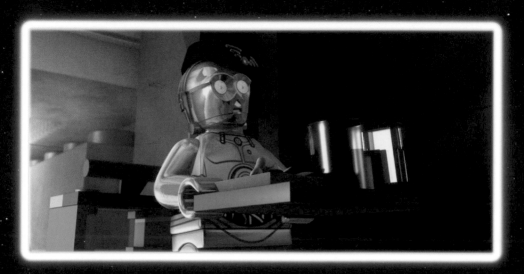

"I must steal a new ship!" Grievous turned to flee. He dashed away, with the Jedi and clone army in hot pursuit. On the landing pad, the general spotted a cruiser and ran for it.

"Welcome aboard, Senator! The galley is stocked for your flight," said a friendly voice as Grievous settled in on board. The general smiled up at a very surprised C-3PO. C-3PO gasped and said, "You're not Senator Organa!"

Grievous grinned. "What was your first clue?"

"Your hideous appearance, if you must know," said C-3PO.

In the nearby Jedi Temple, Anakin and R2-D2 stood before the Jedi Council.

"Still too impulsive, are you. Patience, you still must learn," Yoda was telling Anakin. "Obey the Jedi code, you—"

Just then, Anakin spotted General Grievous sailing by the window of the Temple in the stolen cruiser. He interrupted Yoda. "If you'll excuse me . . ." Anakin powered up his lightsaber and dived through the window. R2 zoomed after him.

"I've got you where I want you, Grievous!" Anakin said. He and R2 clung onto the outside of the ship.

"*Ooh*, I'm shaking in my boots," Grievous said, rolling his droid eyes.

Anakin climbed on top of the ship and poked his head inside the escape hatch. "Permission to come aboard?" Anakin grinned.

Grievous flipped the ship upside down, knocking Anakin off.

"Not granted!" the general screamed.

"We've got to help Anakin," Obi-Wan told the clones. He hopped into his XJ-6 airspeeder. The clones jumped into their speeders and took off after him.

Grievous fired shots at the Jedi speeders. Obi-Wan and the clones fired back.

Meanwhile, Anakin wasn't letting go. Grievous could tell the stubborn Jedi wouldn't give up without a fight. Grievous handed his pilot duties over to C-3PO and climbed out of the ship. He was ready to get rid of Anakin, once and for all.

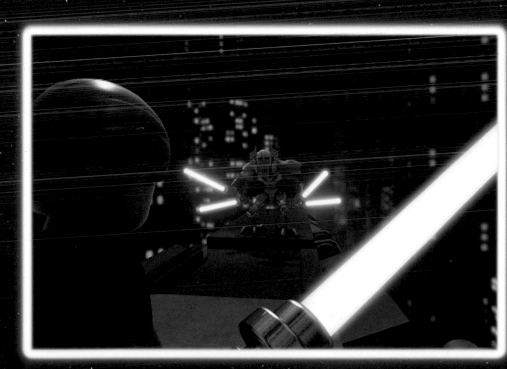

As Grievous and Anakin battled on the wing, C-3PO tried to steer the ship. But he was a terrible pilot! Before long, the giant cruiser was headed straight for a huge building. "Uh-oh," Anakin said, covering his eyes.

Grievous turned and covered his eyes. "Uh-oh."

The ship scraped along the side of the building. Anakin was knocked off. "See ya," Grievous called after him. "Would not want to be ya!"

Anakin tumbled through the sky, screaming. But Obi-Wan swooped in and caught him just in the nick of time!

Obi-Wan smiled at his old Padawan. "You're a full Jedi now, Anakin. You can stop calling me 'Master'."

"Sorry," Anakin said. "Force of habit, Obi."

Obi-Wan cringed. "Uh, let's go back to 'Master'."

"Got it." Anakin nodded. "We'll never find Grievous. Those stolen battle plans are gone forever."

"Not all is lost, my friend," said Obi-Wan. He pointed at the general's cruiser as it zoomed past. "We still have a man on the job."

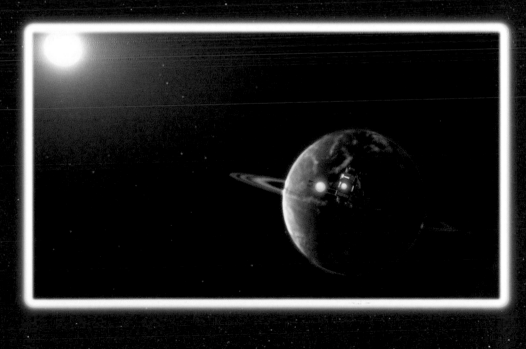

General Grievous flew the stolen ship to the Battle Droid factory on Geonosis. When they landed, he dragged C-3PO out of the ship.

C-3PO looked around and muttered, "Wonderful. From one horrid place to another."

"Come along," Grievous growled. "I have a job for you."

"I can only imagine what degrading task you want me to perform," whined C-3PO.

Neither Grievous nor C-3PO noticed that R2-D2 was following them, waiting for his moment . . .

A short while later, C-3PO was all spiffed up and ready for his waiter duties. "Cocktail sausage?" he said, offering snacks to the leaders of the Separatist Party.

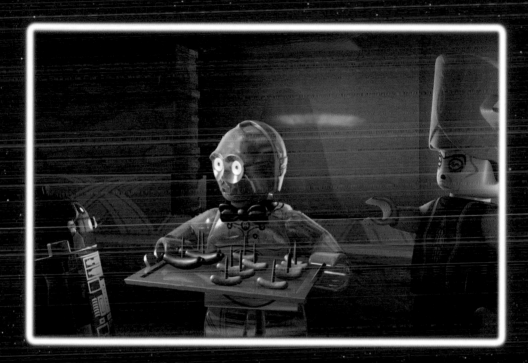

C-3PO turned to a black R2 droid. Something about the droid seemed familiar. Little did he know, it was R2-D2 in disguise!

"Pardon me, but haven't we met before?" C-3PO asked.

R2 beeped and rolled away.

C-3PO sighed. "Probably caught him on a bad day."

R2-D2 parked himself in a corner and aimed his lens at Grievous.

The general handed the disc with the top-secret battle plans to Count Dooku. "Good work, General," said Count Dooku. "These plans will assure our ultimate victory."

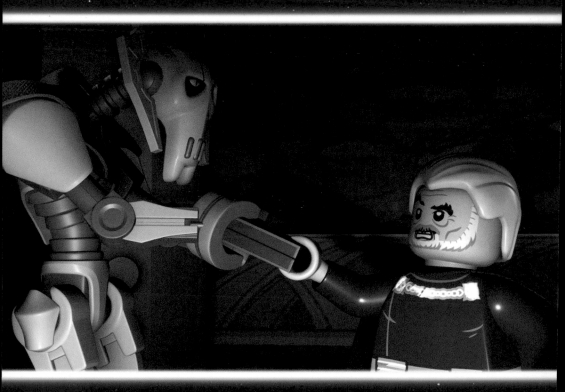

"Yes," agreed General Grievous. "The winning by us is guaranteed."

Count Dooku frowned. "I just said that."

General Grievous shrugged. "I wanted to say it, too!"

FELLOW ENEMIES OF
THE REPUBLIC . . .

Back in the Jedi Temple, the Jedi Council was once again scolding Anakin. Mace Windu said, "Anakin, your effort to stop Grievous was brave, but also reckless. Diving out a window? You could have been killed!"

"Yes, but—" Anakin began.

"No buts!" said Yoda. "Think before you act, you must, if wish to be a great Jedi, you do."

Suddenly, the hologram projector in the centre of the roof blazed on.

"This is coming from Artoo-Detoo!" Obi-Wan gasped. "He's on Geonosis!"

The hologram of Count Dooku held up the top-secret plans and said, "Today . . . we win this war!"

Yoda leapt to his feet. "Get those plans back, you must! Go now!"

Anakin shook his head. "But you just said I have to think—"

"No time to think!" shouted Yoda. "What I said, forget. Go!"

OKAY, MASTER. YOU'RE THE BOSS.

Anakin leapt out the window of the Jedi Chambers. Obi-Wan, Mace Windu, and the other Jedi Council members followed. With a shrug, Yoda jumped, too. "Oh, heck, what the—"

The Jedi raced towards Geonosis while Count Dooku addressed the group of Separatists and Sith Lords. "What I am about to show you will change the course of history." He slipped the top-secret plan disc into R2-D2's projector. "Behold: the secret to our triumph!"

But R2 wasn't about to let them see the secret plans. Instead of displaying the battle plans, he switched the disc and showed them something a little different . . .

"What is the meaning of this, General?" Count Dooku demanded.

But before General Grievous could answer, the Jedi came streaming into the room!

"It means, Dooku," said Yoda, "that up, the jig is!"

"Party's over, boys," said Obi-Wan.

Count Dooku laughed. "Oh, I don't think so.

The battle between the Sith and Jedi was fast-paced and fierce. As lightsabers slashed and hissed, R2 took off his disguise and tried to escape with the top-secret battle plans.

But General Grievous spotted him zooming away. "That droid has the plans!" Grievous and his army of Battle Droids chased after R2. Before long, R2 was surrounded. "Give them to me!"

For one moment, it seemed like there was no way out. But then R2-D2 jumped over the ledge and into the gears of the factory below!

"*Nooo!*" screamed both C-3PO and General Grievous.

C-3PO looked at the general strangely. "Why are you saying '*noooo!*'?"

Grievous cried, "Because he's got the battle plans in him."

"Oh," said C-3PO. "Right. Of course."

C-3PO and Grievous peered over the rail. R2-D2 was jammed between two gears, about to be crushed! But then, R2 pushed the gears apart. Before long, the factory line was stopped up.

"The whole place is going to blow!" yelled Nute Gunray.

Everyone fled from the Battle Droid factory just before it exploded in a mighty blast. The Jedi were all safe . . . and R2-D2 had the top-secret plans!

"Artoo-Detoo, you're a hero!" C-3PO cheered as they sailed away in the Republic Attack Gunship. Then he bonked R2 on the dome. "Never do anything like that again!"

Sighing, C-3PO took a break from telling Admiral Ackbar his story. "I was so mad at Artoo that day. Oh, I hope I see him again . . . so I can give him another smack on the dome!" He slammed his hand down on a pile of crumpled-up posters.

Clang!

C-3PO frowned. "That was an odd sound for paper to make." He began to dig away the mounds of crumpled paper. "Look! This is the ship Artoo was taken away in!"

"*Daisy Mae!*" Ackbar squealed. He ran over

and gave his ship a huge hug. "What have they done to you, kiddo?" The ship had been put back together.

"The spaceport!" C-3PO exclaimed. "Of course! The villain knew we'd follow him, so he ditched your ship for a shuttle ride elsewhere. But where, Admiral? Where?"

"Leave me out of this," Ackbar said. He was busy covering his ship in kisses. "We're re-bonding."

C-3PO rushed to the spaceport ticket booth and shoved other customers aside. When he got to the counter, he asked, "Have you seen my friend? He's a fellow droid, a hero of the Rebellion, and he's been kidnapped!"

"Don't get your gears in a twist," grumbled the ticket droid. "If your friend came through here, he'd be on the security video."

C-3PO watched the security video, but there was no sign of R2. He turned to the other customers in line. "I'm sorry for my rudeness. I'm in a dreadful state. Such a terrible thing to happen to a droid . . ."

Another customer shook his head sadly. "Your friend's a hero. What an awful way to treat some-one who helped defeat the Empire."

"Yes! And the worst part is, it was a kidnap-ping that led to the *rise* of the Empire, the fall of the Jedi, and the Revenge of the Sith in the first place!" said C-3PO.

"Wow," murmured the other customer. "Would you like to tell us about it?"

And so, C-3PO once again began to tell his story of what had happened on Coruscant twenty years earlier. "General Grievous and the Separatists were desperate for a bold move that would end the war," he told the crowd. "They decided to kidnap Chancellor Palpatine . . ."

C-3PO could remember the day as if it were yesterday. After all, he was the only one who was there when General Grievous kidnapped the Chancellor! At the time, he had no idea the whole thing had been a giant set-up . . . arranged by Palpatine himself.

THIS IS A TOTAL SURPRISE KIDNAPPING! HEE-HEE-HEE!

Anakin and Padmé were out for another stroll at the Jedi Temple. R2-D2 trailed along behind them.

"You seem troubled," Padmé said. "Is something wrong?"

Anakin shook his head. "No, just the usual rage at Obi-Wan and Yoda for not seeing my awesomeness." He stopped and took her hand. "But I have a good feeling about us. The future is bright for me, you . . . and our child-to-be."

R2 beeped happily and shot confetti out of his dome – a child for Anakin and Padmé? What wonderful news!

"Thanks, Artoo." Anakin grinned. "Have you thought of a name for the baby yet, Padmé?"

"Well, the girl name is easy: Leia," Padmé said. "For a boy, I've narrowed it down to Kitster, Embo, Wicket, Jubnuk, IG-88 or Luke."

Padmé and Anakin were so busy talking about their baby's name that they didn't notice Chancellor Palpatine waving and screaming from inside General Grievous's ship.

Palpatine honked the ship's horn. That's when Anakin finally looked up and yelped, "The Chancellor's been kidnapped! I have to save him!"

Anakin rushed to his starfighter and called to Obi-Wan on his comlink. "Grievous and Dooku are holding the Chancellor on the command ship."

In no time, the Jedi team was flying towards the command ship. They were ready to save the day . . . and the Chancellor!

Meanwhile, Chancellor Palpatine was trying to come up with his next move.

"Master," Count Dooku said to him, "what a brilliant plan of yours to lure the Jedi to your rescue so you can reveal yourself as the Sith Lord and have us destroy them!"

"Uh, yeah," Palpatine said slowly, nodding. "That was my plan all along!"

Anakin and Obi-Wan burst into the room. "Let him go, Dooku!" yelled Anakin.

"Ha!" laughed Count Dooku. "You just walked into a trap! We have a secret weapon you never suspected." He pointed to Chancellor Palpatine. "The power of the S—"

Palpatine cut him off. "Get those bad guys, my Jedi heroes!"

Count Dooku leaned in and whispered, "Uh, *that* wasn't the plan . . ."

Palpatine shrugged as the Jedi fought Dooku and Grievous. "Yes, it was. I just didn't tell you. Sorry!"

Palpatine watched the lightsaber duel with glee.

When Obi-Wan was knocked out by a pile of bricks, Anakin fought on, two against one. "I'll get you," he growled at the bad guys.

"Yes, Anakin," Palpatine urged. "Give in to your hate!"

"Isn't that a bad thing for a Jedi?" Anakin asked.

"Oh, right!" Palpatine said. "Why would I tell you to do that? Silly me."

With a sudden burst of strength, Anakin pushed both Grievous and Palpatine out of the window!

YOU HAVEN'T SEEN THE LAST OF *MEEEEE!*

YOU HAVE SEEN THE LAST OF *MEEEE!*

Grievous's ship crashed on Coruscant moments later. As he pulled himself out of the rubble, Anakin growled, "Grievous is still out there. I'll hunt him."

"No, Anakin," Obi-Wan said. "*I'll* go. You're not ready!"

"You're just jealous of me," Anakin groaned. "I won't accept this until I hear it from Yoda himself."

Yoda poked his head out of the rubble and said, "Agree with Obi-Wan, I do."

Anakin stormed away. Obi-Wan and Yoda never let him do anything!

Chancellor Palpatine caught up to him and said, "Anakin, you're right to be angry at Yoda. He doesn't see the greatness in you that I do."

"Really?" Anakin asked, perking up. "You think I'm great?"

"Yes." Palpatine nodded. "And I say this from my heart, with no ulterior motives . . ."

Palpatine's face swivelled from good to bad and back again. No matter how hard he tried, his evil side kept popping up to the front. "Gotta go!" he dashed away, trying to hide his face. "Trust me completely, Anakin!"

Anakin watched Palpatine go. Suddenly, he had a crazy idea. "I think the Chancellor is the Sith Lord!"

"Highly unlikely," Mace Windu said with a laugh from nearby. "But I'll check it out."

Obi-Wan tracked
General Grievous to
Utapau.

"I'd love to help you find
this General Grievous. But
he's not here." Tion Medon
jerked his head towards a
column. "No, sir . . . There's
no big scary robot man
lurking behind that column." Medon jerked his
head to the side again.

"Is there something wrong with your neck?"
Obi-Wan asked.

"He's trying to tell you I'm right here! It's one
against four, Jedi!" Grievous
leapt out from behind the
column and waved four
lightsabers in the air.

Anakin knocked
a lightsaber out of
Grievous's hands.
"Ouch!" Grievous
yelped. "No prob-
lem – I'm just as good
with three." When Anakin
knocked out another light-
saber, Grievous groaned. "Wow, you're good.
Good thing I'm the best with two!"

Back on Coruscant, Mace Windu marched into Chancellor Palpatine's office. "You're under arrest, Chancellor. Or should I say . . . *Darth Sidious!*"

Palpatine spun around in his chair and rolled his eyes. "Well, duh." He ripped off his hair, turned his face around, and lifted his hood. Anakin was right: Palpatine and Darth Sidious were the same guy!

"Whoa," Mace Windu gasped. He rushed at Sidious as Anakin raced into the room.

"What's going on?" Anakin demanded.

"Anakin," whined Darth Sidious, "this mean Jedi is attacking poor old me. Help me!"

Anakin was torn. "I don't know what to do." Suddenly, he turned on Mace Windu and knocked the Jedi's lightsaber out of his hand. "Stop hurting my friend!"

Darth Sidious attacked Windu with Force lightning and cackled as Windu fell out of a window. "Congratulations, my friend! You are no longer Anakin Skywalker, second-string Jedi. You are Darth Vader, the most powerful being in the galaxy. Well, except for me. You have to obey my every command."

Back on Utapau, Obi-Wan and his clone troopers chased Grievous. "Ha!" General Grievous laughed as he hopped onto a wheelbike to escape. "*R* means *Real Fast*, right?"

"Sure." Obi-Wan giggled. *R* meant *Reverse* – Grievous was doomed!

Grievous threw the bike into reverse and blasted off the cliff edge backward.

Obi-Wan wheeled around to face the clone troopers. "We won!" But the clone troopers were all flying away in their starfighters. Obi-Wan scratched his head. "Wonder where they're all going?"

When Obi-Wan finally met up with his old Padawan again, he discovered Anakin had gone over to the dark side.

"Anakin," he said, pleading. "I loved you as a brother. But you turned to the dark side and destroyed the Republic!"

Anakin pouted. "I say the *Jedi* were destroying the Republic. The Emperor and I *saved* it."

"You didn't save it!" Obi-Wan scoffed.

YUH-HUH! YUH-HUH!

"Well," Obi-Wan said finally, "as long as it's a fight to the end, let's make it interesting!"

"Agreed." Anakin pulled out his lightsaber. "Last one to the crumbling catwalk high above the lava river is a rotten egg!"

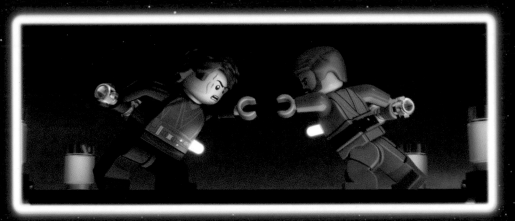

While Obi-Wan and Anakin battled above the lava river, Yoda faced off against Palpatine.

Two battles of good versus evil began that day that would rage on for years.

The battle between Anakin and Obi-Wan was epic. Their powers were evenly matched. The duel finally ended when Anakin lost his footing and plunged into the raging lava river bubbling below.

But Obi-Wan didn't celebrate his victory. Because Anakin Skywalker came out of that battle a new man. That was the day Darth Vader rose to power. Anakin was gone.

Things had never looked worse for the Jedi. But with the birth of Anakin and Padmé's twins, Luke and Leia, there was a new hope for the future.

IN THE PRESENT

"It felt good to talk about that again." C-3PO sighed, finishing his story. "If only I had hope that I would find Artoo—" He broke off, suddenly excited. He pointed at the video monitor behind the ticket droid. "Look! It's Artoo! I'd know that rotating dome anywhere!"

The ticket droid rewound the video so C-3PO could see where R2's shuttle had gone. "Mos Eisley!" C-3PO said. "Artoo's been taken to that wretched stinkhole. I have to save him!"

The ticket droid handed him a ticket just as a spaceport announcer said, "The Tatooine shuttle to Mos Eisley is now boarding on Platform Three."

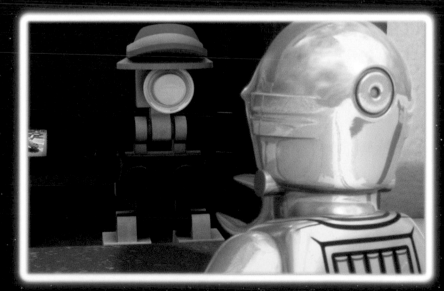

"Thank you for the ride, Admiral," C-3PO called out to Admiral Ackbar. "I must follow Artoo!"

"Of course," Ackbar said. "I'm just happy to have my ship ba—" Ackbar screeched. A Rubbish Droid was towing his beautiful ship away. "Come back here with *Daisy Mae*!"

C-3PO waved to the admiral and hopped on board the shuttle to Mos Eisley. He ran up to the pilot and said, "I can't believe I'm saying this, but . . . take me to Tatooine as fast as you can!"

C-3PO's next adventure was about to begin!